The Day
TIME FROZE

Written by Chris Callaghan

Illustrated by Amit Tayal

Collins

Shinoy and the Chaos Crew

When Shinoy downloads the Chaos Crew app on his phone, a glitch in the system gives him the power to summon his TV heroes into his world.

With the team on board, Shinoy can figure out what dastardly plans the red-eyed S.N.A.I.R., a Super Nasty Artificial Intelligent Robot, has come up with, and save the day.

1 Statues

The kitchen was surprisingly quiet when Shinoy came down for breakfast.

Milo was curled up and sound asleep on the back door mat.

Myra had her head in her books, as usual.

Mum stared out of the window near the toaster. A slice of toast hung motionless in the air.

Wait! What?

A slice of toast hovered above the toaster, like it had popped up and then forgotten to fall back down.

3

"Mum," he said, "look at that!"

But Mum continued staring.
What was she looking at?
A pigeon sat on
the windowsill eyeing up
the toast. Another pigeon,
with wings outstretched,
was suspended in mid-air.
Pigeons don't hover like that,
Shinoy thought.
*Toast definitely doesn't
hover like that.*

"Myra? What's going on? What's up with Mum?"

There was no response from his sister, which was pretty normal.

The clock on the wall said 8:15 a.m. but the time on his phone was 9:08 a.m.

The clock had stopped. Everything had stopped.

5

Shinoy pressed the special Chaos Crew app on his phone to bring his favourite TV characters into his own world. "Call to Action, Chaos Crew!"

Mustang Harry sprang out of a flash of light and bounded around the kitchen. He nodded to Shinoy and sniffed at Milo.

"Greetings friend," he barked, but tilted his head when he got no response. "What's happened to Milo?"

"What's happened to *everything*?" asked Shinoy.

It took Harry a few moments to gather information from his Chaos Crew Data Implant.

"I'm registering a **disturbance in time**!"

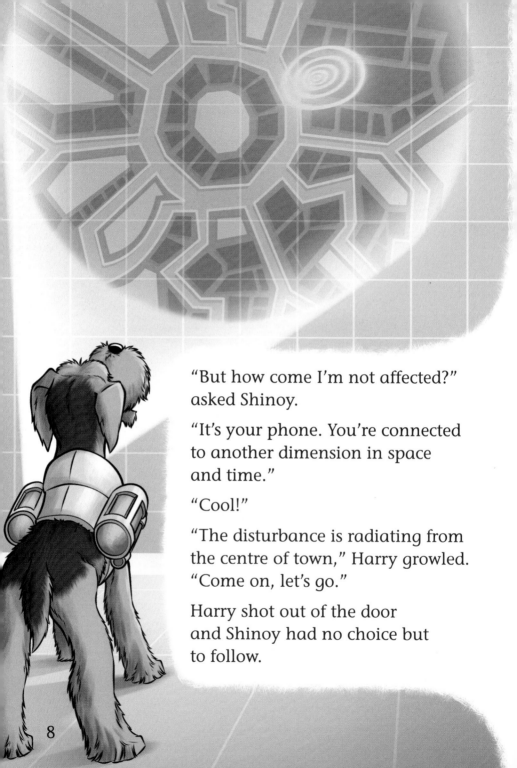

"But how come I'm not affected?" asked Shinoy.

"It's your phone. You're connected to another dimension in space and time."

"Cool!"

"The disturbance is radiating from the centre of town," Harry growled. "Come on, let's go."

Harry shot out of the door and Shinoy had no choice but to follow.

They wove in and out of all the people frozen in time, like statues. It was really weird.

9

On the High Street, Shinoy noticed Sam from the nursing home. He was bending over to pick up some fruit that had spilled out of his carrier bag. Being stuck in that position would give him a bad back, thought Shinoy. He picked up all the loose groceries and returned them into the bag hooked through Sam's fingers.

Further down the street, Shinoy saw Mr Amitri
and his wife. It was strange not seeing him in a suit.
Instead, he was wearing faded jeans and a T-shirt.
And a baseball cap! Mrs Amitri had a large floppy sun
hat – and a thought struck Shinoy. He swapped their
hats around and then raced off before losing sight
of Harry. He couldn't stop chuckling to himself.

2 The countdown

Harry was staring up at the clock tower, which stood tall in the centre of town. Everyone called it Little Ben.

"The time disturbance originates here," said Harry, once Shinoy had caught up. "We need to investigate."

There was a small locked door to the rear of the tower, but it caused no difficulty for the Chaos Crew's battle dog. Harry barged it open with his hefty shoulders and they sped towards the central spiral staircase which led up to the clock face.

13

Sunlight shone in through the clock face showing the time in reverse and lighting up the mechanical wheels and cogs. Like everything else, the hands were still. Harry sniffed around the room while Shinoy grabbed a few much-needed breaths.

A flickering light from a black box caught his eye. It had a digital display with red numbers.

"Does S.N.A.I.R. ever take a day off?" sighed Shinoy.

It read

then

then

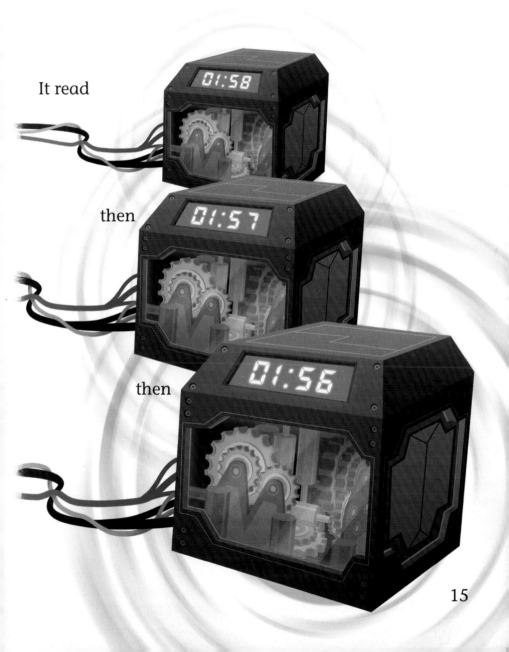

Shinoy and Harry looked at each other in horror.

"It's counting down!" barked Harry.

"Down to what?" asked Shinoy.

Harry's head tilted. "It's a Time Fragmentor. It's already started the first phase, which was to hold time in the present state while it prepares for –" Harry frowned.

"For what?"

"A total time reboot!"

"What? All the clocks will be reset?"

"All of *time* will be reset. Back to its factory setting. To the very beginning."

"Can we get Bug? She could zap it or something.

Or Salama, she could smash it."

Shinoy looked at Harry. "Could you eat it?"

Harry frowned. "Dogs don't eat everything, you know."

"Milo does. Even Dad's sweaty socks."

"There's no time – we need to stop it."

Shinoy looked at the backwards clock face. "Or we could start it?"

Harry barked in agreement. Starting the clock might start time again. Then that could stop the reboot. They had to try. Harry pushed open a small door under the clock face and released a safety cord from his Chaos Crew harness.

3 On the ledge

"Shinoy! Wrap this around yourself and step out on to the ledge."

Shinoy stepped out on to the narrow ledge. He looked down at the town below and gulped hard. He pictured the timer continuing to count down.

He edged along the ledge a bit further.

He reached up to the minute hand of the clock.

"I can't get to it," he shouted to Harry.

00:42

"Stand on me," Harry said, preparing himself to take Shinoy's weight. Balancing on Harry's back, Shinoy stretched on tiptoes and just got his fingertips to the minute hand.

Don't look down, Shinoy told himself, and jumped to get a full grip.

00:26 ...

Dangling high above the town from Little Ben's minute hand was not how Shinoy had expected his Saturday to start!

"It won't budge!" he shouted. Harry bit into the leg of Shinoy's jeans and tugged.

00:13

Shinoy tried to bounce to get it moving. His grip was loosening. Then he felt a sudden short sharp drop. The clock hand moved! Shinoy's grip gave way and he plunged to the ledge.

Harry grabbed Shinoy and held on tight. They heard the sound of whirring mechanisms as the clock started.

Below them, people unfroze. Time had started again!

But was it enough to stop the Time Fragmentor?

Once they were back inside they saw the display.

"*Too* close!" said Harry, while Shinoy whooped with delight.

00:01

4 Defrost!

Harry received a message from his Data Implant. "I'm needed. Can you make your own way home?" Shinoy nodded and Harry disappeared in a flash of light, off on another adventure.

Shinoy enjoyed his steady walk home.

He came across his head teacher again and chuckled, "Nice hat, Mr Amitri."

The embarrassed couple swapped hats quickly. "Haven't you got homework to do?" called out Mr Amitri, as Shinoy ran off.

"How's your back, Sam?" asked Shinoy.

"It's fine thanks, but it's my mind I'm worried about. I could have sworn I'd dropped my … oh, never mind!"

Back home, Shinoy got a friendly welcome from Milo.

"Morning," said Mum. "Nice lie in?"

Shinoy laughed and checked to see if everything had unfrozen.

He looked at Myra. She was perfectly still. *Oh no,* thought Shinoy. Had there been a problem restarting time? He moved closer to examine her face.

"Excuse me," Myra pulled a face, "have you heard of personal space?"

Shinoy laughed. If only he could freeze time right now!

Tick tock!

Ideas for reading

Written by Clare Dowdall, PhD
Lecturer and Primary Literacy Consultant

Reading objectives

- discuss the sequence of events in books and how items of information are related
- discuss and clarify the meanings of words, linking new meanings to known vocabulary
- make inferences on the basis of what is being said and done
- predict what might happen on the basis of what has been read so far

Spoken language objectives

- use relevant strategies to build their vocabulary
- use spoken language to develop understanding through speculating, hypothesising, imagining and exploring ideas

Curriculum links: Mathematics: measurement – telling the time; Art and design – use drawing and painting to develop and share ideas

Word count: 1248

Interest words: motionless, suspended, disturbance, dimension, radiating, originates, fragmentor, reboot, ledge, defrost, unfrozen, restarting

Resources: internet for research, pencils and paper, paints

Build a context for reading

- Read the title *The Day Time Froze*. Ask children to suggest what it might mean.
- Look at the pictures on the front cover and read the blurb together. Discuss what might be happening and challenge children to predict what might happen to Shinoy in the story.
- Introduce the interest words: *motionless, suspended, disturbance, radiating, originates, fragmentor, reboot*. Show children how to look for known words within long words, to help deduce what they mean, e.g. a fragmentor might create fragments. Check children understand the root words within these longer words.